Dealing with

DEATH

GOD'S WAY

Real Answers

For

Real Pain

By Pastor Lee Armstrong

cds@dsheriff.org
www.pastorleearmstrong.com   www.angelsatwar.com

Dealing with Death God's Way, Real Answers for Real Pain
ISBN 978-0-615-35150-6
Copyright application submitted 1/20/2010.
Case/SR# 1-317710301

Published by Angels/Unaware, LLC

Item Code 200

DEDICATION

I would like to dedicate this book to everyone who has endured the painful and often devastating loss of a loved one. To you, I have written this short book, in an effort to bring healing and help in your time of need.

I would also like to thank my pastor Duane Sheriff and all the Victory Life members for their amazing love and support in our times of need. They have been shining examples of how people should respond to those grieving the absence of a precious life.

Finally and with all my heart I would like to express my thanksgiving to my wife and family for showing me in action, many of the truths I have shared in this book!

In Christ,

Pastor Lee Armstrong

Pastor Lee Armstrong

FORWARD

Death is a part of the cycle of life and yet we never seem to be prepared for it when it happens. Few have the knowledge and experience of Pastor Lee and the ability to apply the knowledge that brings comfort to family and friends. With performing hundreds of funerals and untold hours of counseling; Lee has brought healing to many broken hearts. He has been a rock in troubled times that brought stability and peace to rocky situations. This book will not only bring healing and wholeness to many; but it will also equip you to be a blessing and comfort to others.

In Him,

Duane Sheriff

GOD DID NOT TAKE THEM!

Death is the only issue everyone must face. From the death of loved ones to our own eventual demise, we all must learn to deal with this event. The emotions involved make learning more difficult, but only by dealing with death God's way will you receive the comfort you seek.

God's deepest desire is to be loved by His children. Why should children love a father who is responsible for the death of people they cherish? Our Lord is the giver of life, not the taker. Simply put, **God did NOT take your loved one!** As you discover His truth you will find lasting comfort which only comes from the Lord. You will also realize the importance of destroying the works of Satan...the **real** killer.

Satan is a liar, there is no truth in him, and he walks about like a roaring lion seeking <u>whom</u> he may devour (1Peter 5:8). Emotions run high following the death of a loved one and people are easily deceived when emotionally vulnerable. Thankfully, God sent His Word to help us discern all truth.

One of Satan's favorite deceptions is that God takes our loved ones. "The Lord gives and the Lord takes away" is a verse frequently quoted. This comes from the book of Job, describing events which took place before people were even aware of the devil's existence. A closer look reveals that God gave Job the good things he enjoyed, and Satan took them away. Job, his wife and his friends were under many misconceptions, for they were without access to the truth and wisdom we now enjoy through God's Word.

The only thing worse than no information is wrong information and 'God took your loved one' is wrong information. God's very nature is that of a lover and a giver. You cannot place total faith and trust in a God who might kill you at any time. (**John 10:10**) tells us, *"The thief does not come except to steal, and to kill, and to destroy."* We've all heard this verse, but sometimes we pass up the wisdom here as it applies to our circumstance. Believing that God took your loved one allows Satan to accomplish everything described in this verse: 1) someone has been killed 2) your trust in the Lord has been stolen and 3) God's very character and nature has been destructively assaulted. Satan desires for you to blame God because that causes you to pull away from Him. Since Jesus is the healer of the broken hearted, pulling away from Him only deepens your sorrow. The devil can't hurt God but he can hurt your perception of God. By influencing your perception and causing you to suffer he brings grief to the Lord, which is Satan's primary goal.

If you have fallen victim to wrong information the Lord is not angry with you. He does desire, however, that you understand the depth of His love. You wrap Christmas presents and place them under the tree because you desire that your children receive them. In the same way, all the promises contained in God's Word exist because of His desire for us to receive them. In (**John 10:10**) Jesus goes on to say, *"I have come that they may have life, and that they may have it more abundantly."* Throughout God's word He is the giver of life, not the taker. People will say that God took your loved one. Some preachers say this but God's Word does not. God does not take our loved ones, but He will receive them.

In God's Word, we see His genuine love for us. (**Psalm 116:15**) says, *"Precious in the sight of the Lord is the death of His saints."* God cares for you and is touched by anything that touches you. According to the Bible, death is the final enemy to be defeated. God is saddened when any enemy gains victory over you.

WHAT NOW?

There are changes we can make, in both thoughts and actions, which will bring comfort when a death does occur. First we must stop behaving like we are going to live forever. When a husband and wife argue, they assume there will be time to work it out, but what guarantee is there? You never hear someone at a funeral say, "I wish I hadn't spent so much time with dad." Instead, you often hear, "I wish I had spent more time with mom" or "I wish I had made up with my brother." The sad truth is, if you wait until a funeral, it's simply too late.

Tell people how much they mean to you RIGHT NOW. So many nice things are said at funeral services, and those nice things do nothing for the people being spoken about. Encourage someone today by letting them know they've made a difference in your life. One of the greatest forms of criticism is a compliment unspoken. Powerful and lasting change will occur when you increase the frequency of the words, "I Love You."

I am so grateful that the last conversation I had with my daughter was one where my wife and I both told her we loved her and she expressed how much she loved us. We had no way of knowing how soon she would go to be with the Lord. If our last conversation had been filled with bickering and squabbling, we would live with that pain the rest of our lives.

We need to discard the mindset of just enduring "till the sweet by and by." Facing death and seeing it through God's eyes will help you live each day to the fullest. By realizing you are mortal and don't have forever, you learn to enjoy life now instead of waiting for the "by and by." Don't let the devil suggest that "all will be well when you get to heaven." God loves you and He did not place you on Earth just to suffer and endure while you are here. God created all the beauty and riches of this planet for His beloved children to enjoy.

One of the primary riches this life has to offer is family and we need to enjoy that wealth NOW. Loving moments can be shared with family members of all ages. You can engage in deep conversation with young adults and watch them discover the world. Parents are the best friends you will ever have and grandparents are the kindest, least judgmental people you'll know in this lifetime. Each family has its problems yet there is tremendous happiness available. Enjoy family while you have the chance, because little in life will be more rewarding.

MISCONCEPTIONS ABOUT DEATH

One misconception frequently taught is that God only takes the best. In the first place, God does not take He receives. To receive money is good, to take it is theft. The Lord is good, He is not a thief. We're told that good people are brought home by the Lord to receive their reward. While this sounds nice it is an affront to the very nature and character of God. Think this all the way through; if God is taking the best people, why do bad people die? We credit bad people with being products of the devil so maybe he is responsible for bringing his people 'home.' At this point God is killing good people and Satan is killing bad ones. Do you see the flaw in that train of thought and reasoning?

This brand of teaching comes primarily from Job. Remember, Job didn't know there was a devil. For all he knew God was behind the events in his life, but he worshiped God anyway! (**Job 1:22**) states, *"...in all this, Job sinned not." In the second round with the devil (chapter 2) Job was afflicted in his body. This time his wife told him to "curse God and die" yet verse 10 tells us "in all this Job did not sin with his lips."* The Word tells us that it is sin to charge God with evil. Job did not sin. He did not know what was going on, but refused to blame God for the evil in his life. His wife and friends were blaming and cursing God, but Job continued to worship.

Throughout the Bible Satan uses sickness, disease, natural disasters, and other people to afflict the children of God. This was certainly the case in Job's life, yet he "did not sin with his lips." Satan's devices have not changed, he is still responsible for evil yet we blame God for so much of that evil. "God gave me this sickness to teach me a lesson...God caused me to fail in order to humble me...the earthquake was an act of God...God took my loved one." It is my opinion that to say these things is to accuse God falsely. In this way, we are "sinning with our lips."

Satan encourages this mindset because it leaves you with nowhere to go when you are in pain. Running to the one who caused the pain in order to find comfort is foolishness. Satan would love you to turn to drugs or alcohol, because these things will further destroy your life. Don't blame God and run to the devil; blame the devil and run to God.

It will help you to realize that God is not a child abuser. You may say, "Well that is obvious" but is it really? If I had the power to inflict my children with cancer, and I did so, the law would be justified in sending me to prison. We cannot lay the blame for this kind of evil on a loving father. The Lord loves you and wants to heal your broken heart but He is incapable of doing so if you blame Him for breaking it.

Most of the mindless teachings regarding death are meant to give you comfort during a painful time. The thought is nice but no genuine comfort comes from believing a falsehood. Another one of these falsehoods is that God needed another angel in Heaven. It might be sweet to picture your loved one sitting on a cloud playing a harp but this is simply not the case. Angels are too busy to sit around on clouds and your loved one's existence in glory is FAR SUPERIOR to that. God created all the angels that He needs and if a need for more arises He will have no problem creating them. The bottom line is this-when you die, you don't become an angel...you just become dead. The Bible says to be absent from the body is to be present with the Lord and there is an eternal reward, but becoming an angel is not part of it.

So many ridiculous teachings abound in this arena that there is no way I can counter them all. Just to show how silly these teachings get, I will mention one more: and that is; God needed another flower in His bouquet in heaven. If you're unfamiliar with this one, don't think I'm joking, people actually say this. We are

God's children whom He loves; we are not a decoration in heaven. Personally, I don't even like flowers. I certainly don't want to become one. I assure you, God is blessing your loved one with far greater experiences than simply being a flower in His bouquet.

WHERE IS OUR FOCUS?

We act like funerals are about the loved one who passed away, but funerals are supposed to be for us. An air tight casket does nothing to help the person residing in the casket. From fancy bouquets to expensive caskets none of the money spent helps the dead person at all. If you really want to help them, send them some money before they die. If you wish to comfort those who are left behind, send money to them. Spend time with them delivering comfort after a painful loss. Your money and attention is more effective being focused on the person left grieving; not the person who is no longer here and no longer cares.

On a personal note, my wife and I have discussed this and she knows that if I die before her she is free to do what she wants. I won't be here, I won't know, and I won't care. She does know, however, that I would just as soon be cremated and have my ashes scattered in the deer woods. I've told her, "When I'm dead, I will be in heaven receiving my reward. Don't spend $50,000 on a funeral, take that money and spend it on yourself. Take the money and run!"

Why are there often three separate services? Why should we have family night (dragging the family through hurt and pain), the church service (dragging the family through hurt and pain), and then the graveside service (dragging the family through hurt and pain). This is just a tradition which does not have any substance for us today. So much of what we do focuses on tradition, or is on the people who are no longer here. Our focus should remain on the hurting people left behind. The dead do not benefit from our love; their grieving family members do.

IS CREMATION A SIN?

I mentioned my personal desire to be cremated. Some Christians are shocked by this as they are sure cremation is a sin and will send me to hell. Not only will cremation not send someone to hell, it is not a sin. *This teaching comes from* (**Leviticus 18:21** and **20:3-5**). *These passages refer to the pagan practice of offering loved ones up as a sacrifice to Molech. Verse 21 states, "And you shall not let any of your descendants pass through the fire to Molech..."* it doesn't say not to let your loved ones pass through a fire. Theologians differ on their definition of Molech; some say it was a pagan god, others say an ungodly king. Either way, as long as you are not performing a pagan sacrifice by cremating your loved one...you're safe. If cremation were a sin, what would become of Christians who were burned at the stake? Would a Christian fireman who dies while saving someone's life be sent to hell because he died in a fire? Beliefs held solely because of tradition should always be questioned. The Bible ought not to be questioned, but religious traditions should. If your religious traditions don't back up God's Word, throw them out.

IS SUICIDE UNFORGIVABLE?

Another religious tradition says that suicide is a direct ticket to hell. This is one that needs to be thrown out. This belief is based on the question, "Will I die and go to hell if I commit suicide?" The tradition is wrong because the question is wrong. Asking the wrong question will result in the wrong answer every time. The proper question is, "What will send me to hell?" Most Christians believe that sin sends a person to hell, but that is a traditional belief not supported by the Bible. The only thing that sends a person to hell is denying Jesus Christ as Lord. Jesus paid the debt for all sin and is offering that payment to you free of charge. If you reject that payment, the debt will remain yours and payment must be made. Rejection of Jesus sends people to hell, not suicide and not even sin.

People argue, "But you need to have all your sin confessed before you go to heaven, because you can't ask forgiveness after you die." That means someone could be genuinely saved with all sin confessed but dying in a car accident while driving one mile over the speed limit will send them to hell. Don't be ridiculous. Do you really think anyone confesses ALL sin? People aren't even aware of ALL the sin they commit. *The Bible says, "...whatsoever is not of faith is sin"* **(Romans 14:23)**. This means that worrying about anything for even a moment is a sin. I'm not saying this to condemn you, simply to make the point: *Jesus died one time, for all sin, for all time* **(Romans 6:10, 1John 2:2)**. This is good news because no one has knowledge of every imperfection. Just remember, rejection of Jesus sends a person to hell, not sin.

The next question to ask is, "Am I saved?" You may think this is a given, but most people who think about suicide are not saved. This is only true because killing yourself is the result of losing all hope. We serve the God of hope and through salvation, your spirit is joined to that God. Saved people will generally seek Biblical solutions to problems and try to find help rather than just 'checking out early.'

The third question to ask yourself is, "Do I believe the Bible?" *The Bible teaches that your body is the temple of the Holy Spirit and is not your own, having been bought with a price* **(1Corinthians 6:19-20)**. It is wrong to kill your neighbor's dog because that dog belongs to someone else. It is also wrong to kill your own body because that body does not belong to you.

God's Word gives a magnificent answer for suicidal people. The 16th chapter of Acts tells the story of the Philippian jailer given charge of Paul and Silas. Paul and Silas were worshiping God when an earthquake opened all the prison doors. The jailer knew he would be put to death for losing his prisoners so he lost all hope and verse 27 says he "drew his sword to slay himself." In the next verse, Paul gives us the Christian answer to suicide by yelling out, "<u>Do yourself no harm, we are here</u>." The Christian answer to suicide cannot be, "Don't do something stupid" or "Just dial this hotline." The cry of the church to those who have lost hope must be, "Do yourself no harm, we are here!" We need to be there to help people who have lost hope. Paul being there renewed such hope in the jailer's life that he asked, "What must I do to be saved?" This example was recorded in the Bible for a reason. People will be drawn into the Kingdom of God by the hope we have to offer.

ONE LAST QUESTION: WHY?

The last issue which needs to be dealt with is the sad fact that most people think they would feel better if they just knew why a loved one had to die. The simple truth is: knowing WHY will not help you. When a little boy falls from the swing set and cries to his mother, "Why does my arm hurt?" his mother's answer will not stop the pain. Knowing why your loved one is gone will not stop your pain; they will still be gone and you will still hurt.

The human psyche always looks for reason and order. Science tells us that the drive for order is stronger than the drive for food. God made us this way for a reason but the answer you are looking for is not WHY it is WHO. After the death of a loved one there are two WHO's you are looking for. Jesus is one of them because He is the healer of the broken hearted. You need Jesus to comfort you during a time of loss and pain. Jesus lived a human life. Everything we go through was faced and conquered by Jesus. He understands the comfort you need and sincerely desires to help.

The second WHO brings us to the reason people die. Through Adam's transgression Satan was allowed to bring sin into the world. **(Romans 5:12)** plainly states, *"Therefore, just as through one man sin entered the world, and death through sin, and thus death spread to all men, because all sinned..."* People die because there is sin in the world. This explains WHY, which won't help you, but you now know two WHO's, which will. You know who will heal your broken heart as well as who is responsible for breaking it.

Adam is responsible for the transgression but ultimately Satan is guilty of ushering sin into the world. Dedicating your life to destroying the works of the devil will help gain the retribution you crave for the death of your loved one.

Death due to sin can take different forms. Sometimes people die because of other people's sin. When an innocent person is struck and killed by a drunk driver, the death is caused by someone else's sin. If you are old enough to remember the Columbine tragedy you know that the children killed were innocent. These events are tragic and sin is responsible for this tragedy. Some people die because of their own sin. This is the case when a drug addict overdoses. When someone smokes for sixty years and dies of lung cancer, the death was brought about by his own poor choices. Either way, sin is responsible for death and death is never easy on those left behind.

Many people die due to ignorance. Accidentally grabbing hold of a live electrical wire will do it. People die of starvation in India with cows running loose everywhere. Ignorance can kill you.

Another reason people die is explained in **(Hebrews 9:27)**, *"And it is appointed for men to die once, but after this the judgment."* It can come about early due to sin, but it will happen eventually. With all the wonders awaiting us in Glory we shouldn't want to live here forever anyway. Enjoy the beautiful life God gave you and then go to heaven to have an even better life. Looking at it from a Biblical viewpoint, death is a reward for those who lived a life for God.

This brings us to the last reason we die and it is the best reason: so we can receive all the blessings God desires to bestow upon us. In heaven we will 'know even as we are known' so our minds will no longer be a battlefield. In heaven we will no longer need to battle against Satan, poverty, sickness, disease, or taxes. Imagine a life with no Democrats or Republicans. All this is significant because nothing will hinder God from delivering all the wonderful promises that we see in the Bible. **(1Corinthians 15:50)** *says that flesh and blood can not inherit the kingdom of God.* You need to die in order to inherit your reward. When your loved ones die they have everything given to them that you and I are currently trying to attain. All the promises of God are now theirs. There are no more questions and no more hurts. They now have the reason and order which they have been seeking. God sees death as a reward ceremony. This is how dealing with death God's way can help and even bring a form of joy.

It is true that someone you care about has left your life but you did not lose them. You know where they are. You will miss them and your sorrow is justified. The Bible doesn't say not to sorrow; it says not to sorrow as those who have no hope. You know when it is your turn you, will see them again, and this brings hope.

The day before my daughter's life was taken she called me and said, "Dad I'm so looking forward to coming home." We found out later that her life had been taken. The following Sunday the Lord spoke to me saying, "Son, you were waiting for her to come home; she is now waiting for you to come home." Knowing that God did not take her, but He did receive her, has been very comforting for me. My hope is that you find this comfort as well.

So, I'm not in a hurry, but I live each day ready to make the trip. I'm right with God and know that some day I will be in Glory, sharing life with those I love who went before me. It is my sincere desire that this book assists you in receiving God's love during your time of need. I believe truths have been imparted which will help you **"Deal with Death God's Way."**

"SOME WORDS OF ENCOURAGEMENT FOR YOU IN YOUR TIME OF NEED"

*Feeling like you got kicked in the gut?

Psalm 34:18 "If your heart is broken, you'll find God right there; if you're kicked in the gut, he'll help you catch your breath."
{The Message Bible}

Pastors Comment; In your time of hurt and pain God is right there wanted to comfort and console. Jesus came to heal the broken hearted (Luke 4:18). Let Him heal you, run to Him not from Him today!

*Feeling like you've lost what's most dear to you?

Matthew 5:4 "You're blessed when you feel you've lost what is most dear to you. Only then can you be embraced by the One most dear to you"
{The Message Bible}

Pastors Comment; When we are feeling the most empty and abandoned is when we are the most receptive to receive the unconditional love of God. You are the most important thing to God (Zechariah 2:8) the apple of His eye. Let Him fill you today with whatever you need. He will supply!

Feeling like you can't make it through?
Philippians 4:13 "I have the strength to face all conditions by the power that Christ gives me"
{Today's English Version}

Pastors Comment; In our weakness God becomes our strength (2nd Corinthians 12:9). The truth is we don't have the strength to make it through our trials, but that is where God wants to be our strength. We are yoked up to Jesus (Matthew 11:28-30) and He pulls all that we can't!

*Feel like you're separated from God?
Romans 8:38, 39"I have become absolutely convinced that neither death or life, neither messenger of Heaven nor monarch of earth, neither what happens today nor what happens tomorrow," 39 "neither a power from on high nor power from below, nor anything else in God's whole world has any power to separate us from the love of God in Christ Jesus our Lord!"
{Phillips Modern English}

Pastors Comment; This is how wolves attack! They separate the weak from their herd and then bite and devour their prey. The devil is compared a wolf (John 10:11-16) and we must not separate from our family and friends. They help us against the attacks of our enemy the devil!

*Feeling like you didn't receive God's promise?

Hebrews 11:39 "And these men of faith, though they trusted God and won his approval, none of them received all that God had promised them; 40 "for God wanted them to wait and share the even better rewards that were prepared for us." {The Living Bible}

Pastors Comments; It is possible to believe God for something and not receive it and still be in faith! We have to believe that God is more than our personal butler, running around doing whatever we believe for. Live in faith, and if you die, die in faith!

***One final thought;** Romans 14:7-9 "The life and death of each of us has it's influence on others;'
8 "if we live, we live for the Lord; and if we die, we die for the Lord, so that alive or dead we belong to the Lord"
9 "This explains why Christ both died and came to life, it was so that he might be Lord both of the dead and of the living."
{Jerusalem Bible}

"Everyone is going to face death; it is the one inevitable, irrefutable sign that you were alive!"

{Pastor Lee Armstrong}

TESTIMONIALS

"Pastor Lee and the incredible way he lays out God's word in "Dealing with Death God's Way" was instrumental during a difficult time in my life. My aunt had passed away unexpectedly and my family and I were on our· way to her funeral. We were struggling with what the other family members needed to hear and what was the right thing to say to provide comfort. Prior to leaving for the 5 hour trip, I grabbed a copy of "Dealing with Death God's Way". During this trip, we read through this book one page at a time. We drew comfort by what God's word says about this issue but at the same time, we were alarmed about many of the topics we have grown up misinformed about, such as "is cremation wrong", "will God forgive suicide" and much more ..

This book offers clear and concise guidance on what to share and how to share what God's word says about death. Thank you Pastor Lee for being a vehicle whereby. God is using you to educate people so that not only can we be comforted but we can bring the only true comfort provided by the only true comforter, GOD!"

Misti Mosley

TESTIMONIALS

As a recent widow, I was given a copy of Pastor Lee Armstrong's book, "Death God's Way, Real Answers for Real Pain" I was almost afraid to read it. So many books are afraid to speak the truth to the widow, practically encouraging her to wallow in a pity pit for "as long as you need." As I read Pastor Armstrong's book, I gave a sigh of relief. It was short and to the point, backed up with Scripture. Finally, someone has boldly spoken the truth about death. Pastor Armstrong dares to teach the grieving to refocus on the truths about God that we often forget in our sorrow. After reading his book, joy bubbled up inside me. "Death God's Way" clears up wrong thinking and, as such, has rolled back the stone of misunderstanding and misinformation that has crushed far too many widows' already broken hearts. Thanks to Pastor Armstrong, the widow's burden can be lifted, and joy, once again, can be her portion.

Marilee Alvey

TESTIMONIALS

Dear Pastor Lee; I would like to thank you for sending me the Book , "Dealing With Death God's Way". It was such a great comfort to me and my children. My husband Brent took his own life in July and my Pastor's words to me were, "this is a straight ticket to hell". This was so devastating to me as my husband was such a Christian individual and truly lived his life as God intended. Brent was the spiritual leader of our family and truly loved us which was evident in all his actions. Brent touched so many lives with his kindness and generosity. He was diagnosed with pancreatic cancer and suffered greatly for 3 years with what seemed like endless tests, chemotherapy, repeated septic infections, surgeries and repeated hospitalizations. It was very difficult to watch someone that I loved so much suffer in this way. Even though the surgery was considered "successful", the cancer had metastasized to his liver. His memory deteriorated after over a year of chemotherapy to the point that he could not remember things that he had done or needed to do.

Your book really helped me to put things in perspective; we are not on this earth forever and we need to remember that each day is a gift from God. So many of us take for granted that there will be a tomorrow, and how shocking it can be to find out that it is not always the case.

The section on cremation was very significant for me as this was my husbands only request. It was very evident that our pastor did not agree with this request and I needed to know that it was okay honor what Brent had asked of me.

The question" Is Suicide Unforgivable?" has helped me to face each day. This was such a struggle for me because I needed reassurance that my loved one would in fact be in heaven. Brent dedicated his life to using his god given gifts to serve others. To think that he would be condemned after such a life of devotion and ministry was unbelievable to me.

With the help of this book I have learned that a funeral or memorial service is really about "us". Brent did not want an expensive service with all the costly traditions. As you so perfectly describe, he communicated to me shortly after we were married, " I want to be cremated and have my ashes spread in the deer woods".

Thank you so much for the strength and comfort that this book has provided and for helping us to "Deal with Death God's Way."

I have shared this book with others that I have come in contact with who are struggling with various issues surrounding the death of a loved one. Please know that you have touched many lives with your ministry.

God's blessings to you;

Debra from Michigan.

TESTIMONIALS

Pastor Lee:

Thank you, for the opportunity to recommend your book and CD to families that are struggling to cope with a death in their family. As a licensed funeral director for over thirty years, I have witnessed many situations that needed the truth you have compiled in this book. I have heard numerous times a minister repeat that dreaded phrase that "God only takes the best." Your boldness in speaking the truth is refreshing. I believe the truth that God receives their loved one back unto Himself, and His wish is that none should perish, but have life more abundantly. **"Where is our focus?"** Having read and studied many authors throughout the years, and having experienced death in my own family from a funeral directors perspective, I must enlighten you regarding a couple of issues in your text. As you know, the whole concept of funeralization dates back to Egypt, and is of course as you say, for the living and not the dead. Memorialization is a time honored tradition practiced for centuries and serves as a tribute to a life lived. It also provides a focal point for remembrance, as well as a record for future generations.

I have found that each family differs in their response to a death, as well as their response to what ministers to them. Life experience is as different as a life lived. The separate visitation, service, and committal services may seem arduous to some, but yet minister to others. I don't think you can use a cookie cutter funeral service plan and ask a family to fit in the mold, but each family needs the right to make their own decision as to what type of remembrance service fits their family and loved one.

Over the years, I have planned all types of services, from scattering cremains in the mountain streams or out of airplane windows, to mountain Harley rides and wagon carriages back into the woods on the old home place. In respect of this, I do think you may want to re-write your generalization that visitation is a bad thing. Many of those we serve tell us that what they like the best about the services is taking the time to see friends and hear the story of the life lived. Many people work, and in this day and age, do not have the opportunity to take off work for a friends service, so the afterhours visitation gives opportunity for the family to experience the outpouring of love towards them.

Another point that may need correction in the book is the reference to the $50,000 funeral service. Of course, you may have experienced that personally, but living in Oklahoma, families have the opportunity to have quality services at an affordable cost, many times below the national average of $6500 for casket and service. The cost for memorialization is much like a wedding; it could be from nothing, such as donating your body to science, up to whatever you want, including having your cremains blasted into outer space. This reference in your book is also an individual choice by a family regarding the life they are celebrating. I strive to assist families in planning their services within their budget, but yet accomplish all that they want to do in memorialization.

On a personal note, please know, that I am blessed that you have taken on this task of bringing forth the truth.

I just felt you needed to know the rest of the story...

Sincerely yours,

Brent E. Shain CFSP